LITTLE SH...
WANTS TO DO YOGA

Written By Nino Devdariani Farruggio
& Illustrated by Khatuna Devdariani

Published 2017

Book design by Mary Lou Littrell
Printed by CreateSpace, An Amazon.com Company
Available from Amazon.com, other book stores
and Yoga studios

ISBN 978-1532928345

*To all the amazing people in my
life that inspire me to love and to live.
Deepest gratitude to my teacher
Alan Finger,
my mentor Mona Anand and
the entire Ishta Yoga family.
Bottomless thank you to my mother.
Without her this book as well as
my life wouldn't be the same.*

Luca & Nico I love you.

One sunny morning Little Shrimp peeked through the window of the yoga school and saw friends doing yoga. He wanted to do yoga too, but he did not have long arms and legs like his friends.

Little Shrimp had short, tiny, fragile legs that didn't reach as far. They couldn't do things that his friend's arms and legs could do. Little Shrimp started to cry.

After a while, he got tired of crying and took a few deep breaths. Then he had an idea. He decided to ask someone to help him.

Little Shrimp went back to yoga school. The yoga teacher spotted Little Shrimp and came outside to introduce herself. Her name was Guru Turtle. **Guru** means teacher.

Guru Turtle welcomed
Little Shrimp into her **Ashram**,
where Gurus live and teach.
Little Shrimp shared his
predicament with Guru Turtle.
She listened quietly and with
patience. Then Guru smiled.

"Can you breathe Little Shrimp?"
Guru Turtle asked. "Yes, Little Shrimp
replied with a laugh."
"Can you pay attention to your breath
and not think about anything else
for a few moments?" asked Guru.
"That's easy" said Little Shrimp.
"Can you stretch your body?" Guru
Turtle wanted to know.
Little Shrimp tried stretching upward
and felt himself getting a bit taller.
Then he bent over to stretch some
more. "Wow" he said. "I've never
tried that before. It feels good."

"Now feel your heart,"
said Guru Turtle. "Is that what
beats inside my chest?" asked
Little Shrimp. Guru smiled.
"Yes, exactly. Can you feel love
in your heart?"
"Yes, I feel love all the time,"
giggled Little Shrimp.

"Tell me all the things you are thankful for in your life" Guru said.
"I am thankful for my mom and dad, my friends, my home, food in my belly, and toys," replied Little Shrimp.
Guru Turtle patted Little Shrimp's head and nodded.

Then Guru looked into Little Shrimp's eyes and asked, "Do you practice **Ahimsa**?" "What's that?"asked Little Shrimp. "Ahimsa means non-harming in **Sanskrit**. It means to be kind to other living things. Are you kind?" "Yes," replied Little Shrimp quickly. "But what is Sanskrit?" "It's an ancient yoga language," explained Guru.

Little Shrimp was very interested in all that Guru was telling him. But then Little Shrimp remembered why he came.

"Why do you look so sad?" asked Guru. "I still can't do yoga," Little Shrimp said with quivering lips as he tried to hold back tears.

Guru Turtle was not worried. "But of course you can!" she said. "All the things you told me you can do is also yoga.

Doing poses, called **Asana**, is just one part of yoga. Body shape doesn't matter. What matters is that you stretch your body, use your breath, and calm your mind. We all use the body we have in a way that works best for us."

Little Shrimp was so happy to hear that yoga was for everyone! He gave Guru Turtle a big hug and thanked her for being so helpful.

Then Guru had an idea. "Do you wish to start practicing the Asana part of yoga now?"

"Right now?" asked Little Shrimp nervously.

"Yes, now is the only time we can do anything," replied Guru. "Yoga is about learning to be in the now."

Guru invited Little Shrimp to her class and she began to teach. First, Little Shrimp stretched his body. He bent forward and sideways. Then he wiggled his tiny legs around, remembering to breathe the entire time. All this moving and breathing was making him relaxed and a bit tired. Now it was time for Savasana.

Savasana is the final pose of
a yoga practice . Guru said it
was very important to relax and
lie down after each yoga practice.
"Listen to my voice," Guru
said in a gentle, quiet tone. "Feel
and relax your body, your tail,
your legs, your head.
Feel and relax your eyes, your
nose, your mouth. Relax
everything."
Little Shrimp felt very peaceful.

After class, Little Shrimp thanked Guru Turtle. "Remember that things can be done in many different ways," said Guru Turtle. "Any way is fine, as long as it is true to you."
It was a happy day for Little Shrimp. He learned that he could do yoga by accepting himself the way he is. Before they parted, Guru Turtle and Little Shrimp brought their palms together and bowed their heads, whispering a very special word. "**Namaste**," they said to each other. This sanscrit word means... "**The light in me recognizes and honors the light in you.**"

My hope and dream for
this book is that it may reach
the hearts of children of all
ages from 0 to 100+.
I hope it reminds them to
accept and honor their
unique and miraculous selves
with loving kindness.

N.F.

Namaste

Made in the USA
Middletown, DE
29 April 2017